Bossy Flossie

FOR MY **FATHER,**
A BIZ WHIZ WHO KNEW THE REAL
FEELING OF SUCCESS CAME FROM
HELPING THOSE WHO NEEDED HELP.
—SG

FOR **CLARA** AND **ELÉONORE**
—PC-D

PENGUIN WORKSHOP

Penguin Young Readers Group
An Imprint of Penguin Random House LLC

Text copyright © 2017 by Sheila Greenwald. Illustrations copyright
© 2017 by Penguin Random House LLC. All rights reserved. Published
by Penguin Workshop, an imprint of Penguin Random House LLC,
345 Hudson Street, New York, New York 10014. PENGUIN and
PENGUIN WORKSHOP are trademarks of Penguin Books Ltd, and
the W colophon is a trademark of Penguin Random House LLC.
Manufactured in China.

Library of Congress Cataloging-in-Publication Data is available.

ISBN 9780451534309 (paperback)   10 9 8 7 6 5 4 3 2 1
ISBN 9780451534316 (library binding)   10 9 8 7 6 5 4 3 2 1

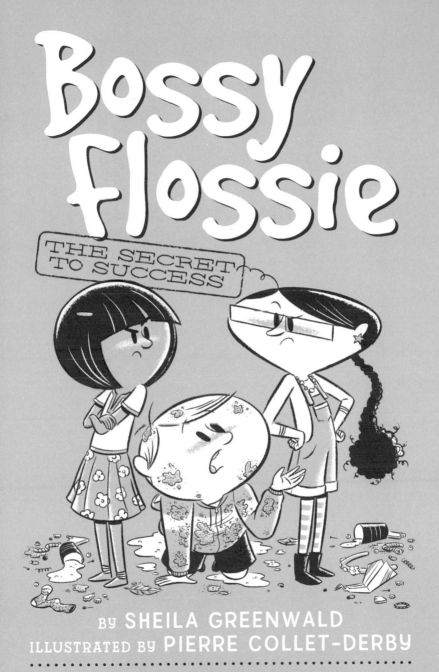

Bossy Flossie

THE SECRET TO SUCCESS

BY SHEILA GREENWALD

ILLUSTRATED BY PIERRE COLLET-DERBY

PENGUIN WORKSHOP ★ AN IMPRINT OF PENGUIN RANDOM HOUSE

THE HOLIDAYS ARE COMING

T he holidays are coming," our teacher, Ms. Cabot, said.

Holiday break was exactly five weeks and three days away. I was keeping track in my planner.

"I bet you're all thinking about eating turkey with your family and opening presents," she said.

"Yes," everyone cheered.

I cheered, too. I had given my holiday present list to my parents.

I was excited about the newest Funny Face doll. I even cut out her picture from a catalog and put it where they couldn't miss it.

"So can you imagine what it's like to have no presents and no home in which to open them?" Ms. Cabot went on.

"Who doesn't have holiday presents?" Imogene Dingle asked.

"Not everyone can afford presents,"

Ms. Cabot told her. "The holidays can be a really rough time for some families."

Everyone was very quiet for a minute.

"Can't anyone help?" Gloria Tubbs asked.

"Yes," Ms. Cabot said. "Every year our school holds a charity drive. I bet our class can think of ways to raise money that will make the holidays better for a lot of families."

"A bake sale," Lulu Marx called out.

"We could go door-to-door in our buildings asking for donations," Daphne Gomez suggested.

"Wonderful ideas," Ms. Cabot said, writing them on the board.

"I'm sure you'll come up with even more when you think about it. After that we'll divide into groups. Each group will have a booth at the school charity drive next Monday."

"I've got a great idea for a booth," Imogene whispered to me while Ms. Cabot handed out flyers telling the time and date of the fundraiser. "It will raise the most money."

I guessed Imogene was lying and didn't have a single idea for a booth yet. Neither did I. But, lucky for me, great ideas and making them happen are what I'm best at.

THINKING ABOUT IT

My name is Flossie Popkin, and as I said, great ideas are what I'm best at.

Though I have brown hair like my dad and it's curly like my mom's, the person I take after most is my Great-Grandpa Morris, who was bald.

Great-Grandpa was famous for dreaming up successful businesses. I'm not famous yet, but I've dreamed up a lot of businesses. Every time I get

a great idea for one, I start to *tingle and glow* from head to toe.

I wondered if Great-Grandpa *tingled and glowed* from head to toe every time he came up with one of his ideas.

But at lunch, I wasn't *tingling and glowing*, at least not yet. I needed to come up with my next great idea.

Gloria also did not look happy. She could hardly eat her lunch.

"Those poor kids who have no gifts," she said with a sigh. "It's so sad."

"My parents always give us holiday presents," Daphne said. "It wouldn't seem like a holiday without them. I want a Funny Face doll this year," she told us. "They're the best."

"The best are the dolls my mom makes out of socks and beads," Imogene disagreed. "I've got tons."

"Then you should donate some to a charity drive toy booth," Daphne suggested.

"If I did that, they'd be gone in a

minute," Imogene boasted. "But we can't give them away. Every year my mom sells them at a holiday craft fair in our living room."

"Can I help?" I asked. "I'm great at selling. I had a lemonade stand and a vegetable sale. I even had a beauty parlor."

"I know all about the beauty parlor," Imogene reminded me, pointing to her head.

"Cutting curly hair is harder than I thought," I said. It felt like the millionth time I had apologized for the Mohawk I gave her by mistake.

"A lemonade stand on the sidewalk or haircuts in your kitchen are not the same as selling handmade dolls,"

Imogene snapped. "We even serve punch and cheese with crackers."

"Don't serve crackers," I advised. "They make a mess. I would know. I'm great at snacks."

"You're great at bossing everybody around," Imogene muttered. "Bossy Flossie. Who could work with you?"

"Me!" Billy Lark shouted from the other end of the table.

Imogene rolled her eyes. "That's because you live in Flossie's building," she scoffed.

"It's because we're partners," Billy protested. "Our vegetable stand at last year's Street Fair Fundraiser was a hit."

"Billy is ready for my ideas," I told Imogene. "Some people aren't."

"Some people aren't ready for you, Bossy Flossie," Imogene said.

"Bossy Flossie, Bossy Flossie," Imogene's friend Charlie Diaz teased.

"Bossy just means I know how to make things happen," I told Charlie.

"So what are you going to make happen next?" Imogene asked.

"Coming soon," I said, because I didn't know yet.

3

COMING SOON

I don't have anything to sell, and nobody will buy my mom's sugar-free cake," Billy complained on the way home from school.

Billy and I were friends, ever since everyone in our class except me made fun of him for talking about super-healthy food all the time.

"We'll think of something," I assured him.

Just then I saw Willow Tipton and

her nanny, Ms. Moss, stepping out of a taxi.

"Willow lives in the biggest apartment in our building," I told Billy.

"Lucky Willow," Billy said.

But Willow didn't look lucky.

She had an ice pack on her arm, and I could see some bandages, too.

"No more trips to Dr. Max." Willow wept as we followed her through the lobby and into the elevator. "It's not fair that I go to see him for an earache and come home with an elbow ache."

"You didn't notice the steps into his office and fell down," Ms. Moss said, soothing Willow as she patted her shoulder. "You'll feel better soon. Dr. Max says your ears are all better and you'll be having fun with your friends in no time."

"I don't have any friends," Willow grumbled as she stepped out of the elevator.

"Willow was in our class last year,"

I told Billy. "She had bad earaches and had to stay home. In school she cried so much Charlie Diaz called her Weeping Willow."

"He called me Cabbage Head," Billy reminded me. "Poor Willow. Nobody wants to be friends with you when you have a nickname like that."

"Except me," I said. I knew how Willow felt.

4

COMFORT SOUP

The reason I wanted to get to know Willow was that until Billy came along, I had no friends at school either. I was sorry Willow stopped coming to school.

When I got home, my mom and my brother, Simon the science whiz, were in the kitchen.

Simon was mixing food for his pet rats, Mr. Salt and Mr. Pepper, and a new family of mice he bought

at the pet shop. Mom was stirring
a pot at the stove.

"Since Dad and I are on the late
shift at the hospital, you and your
brother can just heat this up for
dinner," she said. "It's my comfort
soup."

"I know who could use some comfort soup," I said.

"Who?" Mom asked.

"Willow Tipton. I just saw her get out of a taxi. She fell down at her doctor's office. She was crying."

"Soup for Willow, what a good idea," Mom said. She handed me a jarful.

"Maybe Willow would like a comfort mouse," Simon offered. "I've got six babies to spare."

I said no to the mouse but put the soup in a paper bag and took the elevator down to apartment 7A.

"My mom made her special comfort soup, and I thought you might like some," I told Willow

when she and her nanny opened
the door.

"How lovely, Willow!" her nanny
gushed. "You have a friend in
the building who has come to see
you."

"She didn't come to see me,"
Willow grumbled. "She came to
see my toys."

"Why would I do that?" I asked.

"Because everyone knows
Mom and Dad own Tipton's Toys
for Tots, and I've got more toys
than Santa." Willow opened the
door wider for me to come inside.
"I'll show you."

When we got to her room, I was
amazed.

"It's like Toys 'R' You," I joked. "Why are they all still in boxes, though?"

"Because I don't like toys," Willow declared with a shrug.

"How could you not like toys?" I

asked. I could see at least three Funny Face dolls. I just wanted one.

"They're no fun," Willow said.

"Maybe that's because you need someone to help you play with them," I suggested.

"I don't like playing either," Willow said.

"If you don't like playing with your toys, maybe you could give them to someone who does," I said. "Today at school we were talking about how some kids don't get any toys, even for the holidays."

"They can't have mine," Willow snapped. "I don't like dolls or games. But if I didn't have them, no one would ever visit me."

"What about those?" I asked, pointing to the shelf full of craft kits. "They look like fun."

"Fun?" Willow burst out laughing. "Who needs twelve pot holders, twenty felt tote bags, fifteen doodle socks, twenty macramé rings, five beaded rubber-band bracelets, twenty duct-tape belts, or fifteen glow-in-the-dark creepy crawler rubber worms?" She took a deep breath. "What would I do with all that stuff?"

"I know what to do with it," I said.

"What?"

"Sell them from a craft booth at our school's charity drive to help needy families."

"A craft booth?" Willow repeated.

"Join our team. We'll help you make them. Everybody loves to buy crafts. Next Monday we'll have the best booth at the charity sale."

Willow's eyes grew wider and wider. "I would like that," she whispered.

"Like what?" her nanny asked.

"Crafts by Willow," Willow cried excitedly.

"You mean Crafts by Ms. Cabot's Class to raise money for needy families to celebrate the holidays," I corrected her.

Willow began to rub her ear. "But I'm not in Ms. Cabot's class," she said. "I do my schoolwork at home. I'm sick."

"Dr. Max says you're fine," her nanny disagreed. "He says you could go back to school tomorrow."

Willow tugged on both ears.

"You're making my ears hurt," she accused me.

"I'm sorry," I apologized. "I didn't

know your ears would hurt if you made crafts with a team and sold them in the best booth ever at our school fundraiser."

"The best booth ever?" Willow let go of her ears. "I think they just stopped hurting," she said.

I had a feeling I wasn't the only one *tingling and glowing* from head to toe.

CRAFT FAIR

Mom was putting on her coat to go to work when I came home from Willow's.

"Your cheeks are pink and shiny," she said. "Do you have a fever, or are you starting a new business?"

"Not a new business, a craft sale booth to raise money for a needy family." I showed Mom the flyer that Ms. Cabot had given us.

"What a wonderful idea!" Mom

exclaimed. "Every day in the hospital I see sick people and their children whose lives could be changed by charity help like that." She gave me a big hug.

"Great-Grandpa Morris told us he was so proud of me and Dad when we took up nursing. He believed helping others was the secret to success."

"Helping others is the secret to success? What about publicity and promotion and presentation and location and opportunity? What about winning out over everybody else in business?" I asked.

"There's more than one way to win," Mom said.

That didn't make sense. Winning was winning. Winning meant selling more stuff and raising more money than Imogene or any other booth at our charity sale.

I was glad I understood Great-Grandpa's other advice.

It was pinned on the bulletin board over my desk.

GREAT-GRANDPA'S ADVICE

1. When opportunity knocks, open the door.
2. Publicity Is Gold.
3. If plan A doesn't work, there's always plan B.
4. Location, location, location.
5. Right time + right place = Winner.

I called Billy to tell him about Willow and her craft kits.

"I love making paper planes," he said. "But don't ask me to use glitter glue. I hate glitter glue."

I promised Billy he wouldn't have to use glitter glue. He seemed excited to join a crafting project.

But the next morning on the way to school, Billy's nose began to twitch. Whenever Billy's nose goes up and down like a rabbit's, I know he's worried about something.

"Can we use Willow's craft kits if she isn't in our class anymore?" he asked.

"She'll be back soon," I assured him.

Billy didn't look assured. He was worried for the whole walk, and right up until Ms. Cabot asked us about our project.

But when Ms. Cabot said, "A craft booth is a great idea, Flossie and Billy," he gave me a high five.

Ms. Cabot added our craft sale booth to the list on the board along with "Bake Sale" and "Toy Sale" and "Book Sale."

"I've got some macramé bracelets I could give you," Lulu told me.

"I have some clay pots," Daphne said.

"What if we don't have any crafts to offer?" Charlie asked.

"No problem," I told him. "Just meet us after school. We've got tons of kits to work from."

"I love craft kits," Gloria gushed.

"This is going to be such a fabulous charity sale," Ms. Cabot said. "Be sure to bring in your items to sell on Monday morning and tell your friends. The more people who come, the more money we'll raise."

"I'll post flyers in my building," Daphne piped up.

"I'll tell my soccer team," Imogene said.

Wow!

Flyers and a whole soccer team.

Great-Grandpa would be proud.

We had opportunity and publicity and location. We couldn't lose.

On the way home from school, Gloria and Billy raced each other. I ran with Charlie, trying to catch up. I couldn't wait to start.

FACTORY

But when we rang Willow's doorbell, she wouldn't let us in.

"Who said you could bring a crowd?" she complained.

"It's just four people." I counted again to be sure. "Me, Billy, Charlie, and Gloria. If we're going to make enough crafts in time for a craft booth at the fundraiser, we need a crowd," I explained.

Willow thought about this for a minute.

"I have an idea," she said with a smile. "My mom and dad told me all about how products are made for Tipton's Toys."

She led us into the dining room. On the table were stacks of craft kits.

"We need a factory," Willow said. "Here's how it works."

After she arranged chairs around the table and told us each where to sit, she held up a plain headband to demonstrate.

"I'll paste on the feathers and pass it to Gloria to do the stones. Gloria will pass it to Flossie for the beads.

Charlie and Billy can finish with glitter glue."

"I don't like glitter glue," Billy said.

"You have to listen to me," Willow insisted. "I know how factories work."

"I know how business works," I said. "Crafts that look exactly the same won't sell."

I picked up one of the headbands. "Gloria, you can start on the purple headband," I said, handing it to her. "Billy, you can do green, and Charlie—"

"I want to make paper planes," Charlie interrupted me. He reached under the stack of crafts for the box with the paper parts to cut and fold.

"My great-grandpa owned a toy factory," Willow shouted. "An assembly line is the fastest way to produce a finished product."

"My great-grandpa worked in a factory," Gloria told her. "When the bosses got too bossy, he and the other workers went on strike."

"What's a strike?" Billy asked.

"If the boss isn't fair, the workers get together and walk off the job," Gloria said.

"Who said a boss was supposed to be fair?" Willow asked. "A boss is supposed to be bossy. A boss is supposed to make sure you get the work done."

"I don't want to get work done in

a factory," Charlie announced. He stood up and put on his coat.

"Me neither," Gloria said. She took her jacket and followed him to the door. So did Billy.

"Don't forget the kits are mine!" Willow yelled after them.

"Don't forget," I said quietly, "the team is ours."

I joined the rest of our team by the elevator. Billy's nose was twitching, and Gloria was shaking her head. Charlie pushed the button for the elevator ten times in a row.

Willow watched us from her door.

"This team is giving me an earache," she groaned.

"The doctor said your ear is better," I reminded her. "You could go back to school."

"Why should I go back? No one liked me. I never had any friends there," Willow whimpered.

"And now I know why," I said.

"You're as bossy as Flossie," Gloria told her.

The elevator door opened. Charlie, Gloria, and Billy stepped in and waited for me.

I stepped into the elevator and looked back at Willow.

She was wrong to insist on an assembly line and wrong to say the team gave her an earache, but Gloria was right.

"We do have a lot in common," I told her.

"We do?" she asked me.

"Yes," I said. "But you don't know much about how to run a business."

Willow took her hands off her ears and walked over so she could stop the elevator door from closing.

"Come back," she told us. "No more assembly line."

We all stepped out of the elevator and followed Willow back into her apartment. There was a lot of work to do.

7

BAD NEWS, GOOD NEWS

No wonder your mom loves making crafts," I told Imogene first thing in the morning. "Working with Willow's craft kits is so much fun."

"*Willow's* craft kits?" Imogene gasped. She waved her hand in the air. "Ms. Cabot, Ms. Cabot," she called out, "is it fair that Flossie's team is using Willow's craft kits if Willow isn't even in our class?"

Ms. Cabot thought about it. "Willow needs to be in school to be part of a booth at the charity drive," she decided. "Let's all hope she's back soon."

"She will be," I assured everyone.

"Until she's in our class, I'm not making crafts at Willow's anymore," Gloria told me. "I want to be part

of a booth that raises money at the charity drive."

"Me too," Charlie agreed. "I'm done with crafting."

After school, Billy and I walked home alone. When we rang the doorbell at Willow's, she was surprised.

"Where is everyone?" she asked.

"Ms. Cabot said you have to be in school to be on our team," I said.

Willow began rubbing her ears.

"They hurt," she whined. But from the way she looked, it wasn't just her ears that were hurting.

"What would your great-grandpa say now?" Billy asked me after Willow closed the door on us.

"If plan A doesn't work, there's always plan B."

"What's plan B?" Billy asked.

"I have to think about it," I said.

And so I thought and I thought.

The next morning, I waited at the elevator to tell Billy the bad news.

"There's no plan B," I said as soon as the elevator door opened.

Only the person who stepped out
first wasn't Billy. It was Willow.

"I'm going back to school," she said.

When we walked into the classroom,
Ms. Cabot made an announcement.

"Let's all welcome back Willow,"
she said.

"Welcome back, Willow!" everyone
shouted.

I didn't think anyone would call
her Weeping Willow ever again.
She couldn't stop smiling.

When we left school, Willow ran
ahead of the team, even faster than
Gloria.

"Speed it up," she shouted. "We
have a lot to do."

Willow's nanny brought in a tray of cocoa and cookies, but we hardly had time to eat or drink a thing. We were working hard to finish every item in every craft kit on the table.

Before we left Willow's, Gloria counted up what we had done.

"We're ready for the sale on Monday," she said.

"Too bad they say there's a blizzard heading our way on Sunday," Willow's nanny said. "But weatherpeople are often wrong."

WEATHERPEOPLE ARE NOT WRONG

On Sunday morning, Mom looked out the window. "Who would go out on a day like this?" she asked.

"You and me," Dad told her. "It's our shift at the hospital, blizzard or not."

"Hooray, blizzard!" Simon cheered. "Snow day tomorrow."

"Snow day tomorrow?" I wailed. "It's Charity Drive Day!"

Willow called. She was crying.

"Monday is a snow day," she wept. "Mom and Dad are stuck at the toy fair in LA. My nanny's stuck home with a cold. I'm stuck with her daughter, Patsy, and a load of crafts and no charity booth to sell them at."

She was crying so hard she couldn't catch her breath.

I had to think of something.

"Remember, when plan A doesn't work, there's always a plan B," I said.

"What plan B?" Willow sobbed.

I searched Great-Grandpa's words of advice on the bulletin board over my desk.

Right time + right place = Winner.

"Don't worry," I told Willow. "We have a winner."

In my closet I found a piece of poster board left over from my lemonade stand and got to work on plan B.

I guessed Willow's sitter Patsy would say no to my plan B taking place at Willow's since she didn't have permission from her parents.

So I was glad when Mom told Simon he was in charge before she and Dad left for work.

But when I showed him my sign, he shook his head.

STUCK INSIDE IN A BLIZZARD WITH NOTHING TO DO? DON'T DESPAIR

CHARITY CRAFT SALE
TO RAISE MONEY FOR NEEDY FAMILIES

Time: Noon   Place: Apt 9C.
Bring Food. Bring yourself.

"No way," Simon said after he read it. "If anything goes wrong, it will be my fault."

"Patsy's too," I said.

"Patsy?" Simon asked. "Patsy who?"

"Willow's nanny is sick, so her daughter is there instead."

Simon's frown turned to a smile. "Patsy's in my class," he realized.

I knew she was. He talked about her a lot.

"Actually, what could go wrong with a craft sale? Maybe it's a great idea," Simon decided.

"It *is* a great idea," I agreed. "The craft sale booth we planned for was supposed to happen on Monday. But Monday is a snow day. If we hold a sale now, we'll raise money for charity even though school is closed."

When Billy and Willow heard my plan, they were excited.

When Patsy heard my brother Simon was in charge, she was thrilled.

Simon printed out our flyers on his computer.

Billy distributed copies to apartments in the building. Willow and I hung the sign I made in the lobby.

"Let's not show all our crafts," I told Willow. "In case the charity drive at school is put off for another day we'll need some to sell."

"It looks nicer if the table is full," Willow disagreed.

"Too much stuff on display makes everything look cheap," I said. "I know something about presentation."

"I know about presentation, too," Willow barked. "Remember, my parents own a toy store."

"Remember *I've* owned a lemonade stand, a beauty parlor, and a vegetable stand."

"Remember, the crafts are mine," Willow said.

She dumped out all the boxes onto the dining room table.

I wanted to put some back, but it was too late. The doorbell was ringing.

CRAFT FAIR TIME

There stood Ethan Schuster from the tenth floor with his mom, and the Foster sisters, Emma and Anna, with theirs. The Herman twins, Coco and Calvin, were with their dad.

Patsy and Simon gave everyone a glass of apple juice. The craft fair was off to a good start.

"This is great," Mr. Herman said. "Getting stuck indoors all day is no fun."

"It's so nice to see other kids from the building," Ms. Foster said. "And it's lovely that you're selling your crafts for a good cause."

"Ethan, do you want anything?" Ms. Schuster asked her son.

Ethan shrugged. Coco and Calvin started digging through the pile of crafts on the table.

"Since you have two babysitters here, I'll zip up to my place," Ms. Schuster told Patsy and Simon. "I've got a load of laundry to take care of. When I pick up Ethan, I'll pay for what he has bought."

"I have a stack of papers to go through," Ms. Foster told Emma and Anna. "Just select what you want and I'll be back with my wallet."

"While you pick something out, I'll go home to check on my mail," Mr. Herman told the twins.

The parents left without finishing their apple juice.

As soon as they were gone, Simon and Patsy went to feed the mice.

I clapped my hands for attention.

"The charity craft sale is open,"
I announced.

Calvin picked up a glow-in-the-dark
worm and started wagging it in his
sister's face.

"That's five dollars," I told him.

Coco picked up another worm and
started shaking it, too.

"Careful," I said. "We worked really
hard on those."

Anna selected a duct-tape belt, but
Emma said she touched it first and
pulled it out of her hand.

"There are nineteen more of those,"
Willow said. "You don't have to fight over
that one."

Emma ignored her and kept tugging
on the belt to get it away from her sister.

Calvin and Coco were hitting each
other with handfuls of worms. Ethan
stacked all twelve headbands on his
head and walked around trying to
balance them.

One headband fell over his eyes,
so he couldn't see. He bumped into
Calvin, who fell against Coco. A worm
landed on Anna's head, and suddenly
everyone was screaming and shoving.

Before I could do anything, the table tipped.

Beads, glitter glue, and apple juice were all over the rug.

I ran to Simon's door and banged on it.

"Help!" I hollered.

Simon opened his door, saw the mess, and got a mop. Patsy tried to calm Anna, who was screaming because she had glow-in-the-dark worms stuck in her hair.

Billy had glitter glue all over his shirt. "I hate glitter glue," he said.

"I hate messes," Simon said. He mopped up apple juice on the floor and went to get the vacuum.

Everything was ruined.

The doorbell was ringing again, and the parents were back.

"Sorry it took so long," Ms. Foster said. "What did my girls pick out to buy?"

"There's nothing to buy," I told her.

She looked down at the twelve headbands, fifteen glow-in-the-dark worms, seven food-fight sets, apple juice puddles, and glitter on the floor.

"Oh, sad," she said.

"So sad," Ms. Schuster agreed.

"Sad, sad," Mr. Herman repeated.

"What's really sad is the money we never got to raise for the families in shelters and hospitals, and the children who won't get presents for the holidays," I said.

"No presents for the holidays?" Coco asked.

"Some kids don't get any," I told her. "If we had crafts for you to buy, we could have made a difference. They would have had presents for the holidays. But now they won't get anything."

As we watched our customers troop out the door with not a single sale, I tried to think of something Great-Grandpa said that could cheer up my team.

I had tried helping others, but that wasn't the key to success. It seemed as if helping others was the key to apple juice all over the floor and Billy covered in glitter glue.

WIN SOME, WIN SOME

Tuesday morning the snow was cleared. Willow's mom and dad were back from LA. Tipton's Toys for Tots was open. So was school.

"Since we couldn't have the charity drive on Monday, it will take place tomorrow," Ms. Cabot announced first thing.

"I'll need a shopping cart to bring in all the toys I've collected for the toy

booth," Imogene bragged. "I've got tons."

"So do we," Gloria boasted. "Tons and tons."

Charlie and Gloria sang out, "Go craft team."

Billy's entire face began to twitch.

Willow pulled on both ears.

"Our team has a problem," I told Gloria and Charlie.

After I clued them in on "the problem," they were not happy.

"You should have told us you were having a sale on Sunday!" Gloria scolded me.

"We thought there wouldn't be any school sale," I explained. "We thought at least we'd sell something."

"So, Bossy Flossie, you made your great idea happen, and your great idea was a great big flop," Charlie growled.

After a moment, Billy began to sputter. "If p-plan A doesn't work, there's always p-plan B," he said.

"Are there any crafts left that weren't too damaged?" Charlie asked.

"We didn't throw anything away," I said. "Let's check."

After school, our team met to search through the bag of ruined crafts.

"My headbands are a mess," Gloria moaned.

"But the worms are okay," Charlie reported. "I could add some fresh paint."

"The paper planes are all sticky from apple juice," Billy said. "I guess I could clean them off."

We set aside whatever we thought we could sell. There wasn't much.

Gloria began to cry.

We were all so sad we hardly heard the doorbell ring.

It was Ethan and Coco and Calvin and Emma and Anna with their parents.

Their arms were full.

"I'm sorry we ruined your crafts," Emma said.

"When you told us you didn't have anything to sell, we felt bad about the people in the hospitals and the shelters who we didn't help."

Ethan shook out the change and bills in his piggy bank. "My allowance," he said.

"Mine too," Coco said. She emptied a box of money on top of Ethan's pile.

"We're getting new toys and books for the holidays, so someone might like these," Anna told me. She set down a bag full of dolls and games.

"We wish they were new," Emma added.

"But Ms. Cabot said we can't sell used toys," I said. "It's on the instructions."

"Don't worry about that," Willow said very slowly as if she were about to announce a great, new idea.

"Why not?" I asked.

"Because I have tons of new toys to give to the toy booth at the charity sale," she said.

As soon as Coco and Calvin and Emma and Anna and Ethan left with their parents, I grabbed Willow by the arm.

"Are you really giving away all your toys?" I asked.

"I never liked them," Willow said.

"But we can't sell them at our booth," Gloria said. "We have a craft booth. These are toys."

"Imogene has the toy booth," Willow said. "She could sell our toys."

All four of us were quiet for a minute.

"With these donations, Imogene's

toy booth will be tomorrow's big hit at the charity drive," Charlie realized. "She'll be the winner."

"Maybe there's more than one way to win," Billy said.

Suddenly I began to *tingle and glow* from head to toe. "That's it!" I cried.

"What's it?" Billy asked.

"My great-grandpa's secret to success," I shouted.

"It's not a secret anymore," Charlie said. "We all found out how it feels to help."

He sent a paper plane flying right up to the ceiling. "It works," he cheered.

And we all joined in.